Thunderstorms

by Matt Doeden

Lerner Publications Company • Minneapolis

Photo Acknowledgments

The images in this book are used with the permission of: © Photodisc/Getty Images, pp. 1, 12, all backgrounds; © Royalty-Free/CORBIS, p. 4; © A. T. Willett/Alamy, pp. 6, 18; © NASA/Corbis, p. 7; © Ethan Janson/Lifesize/Getty Images, p. 8; © Thomas Wiewandt/Taxi/Getty Images, p. 9; © Jim Reed/CORBIS, pp. 10, 15, 20, 24; NOAA Photo Library; OAR/ERL/National Severe Storms Laboratory (NSSL), p. 11; © Dennis Hallinan/Alamy, p. 14; © Paul A. Souders/CORBIS, p. 16; © age fotostock/SuperStock, pp. 21, 22; © Michael Bradley/Getty Images, p. 23; © Bob Pardue/Alamy, p. 26; © Mike Magnuson/Riser/Getty Images, p. 27. Illustration on p. 28 by © Laura Westlund/Independent Picture Service.

Front cover: © Florian Werner/LOOK/Getty Images
Back cover: © Photodisc/Getty Images

Lerner Publications Company
A division of Lerner Publishing Group, Inc.
241 First Avenue North
Minneapolis, MN 55401

Website address: www.lernerbooks.com

Words in **bold type** are explained in a glossary on page 31.

Library of Congress Cataloging-in-Publication Data

Doeden, Matt.
     Thunderstorms / by Matt Doeden.
         p.   cm. — (Pull ahead books—forces of nature)
     Includes index.
     ISBN 978-0-8225-7908-3 (lib. bdg. : alk. paper)
     1. Thunderstorms—Juvenile literature. I. Title.
QC968.2.D64 2008
551.55'4—dc22   2007024904

Manufactured in the United States of America
1 2 3 4 5 6 – JR – 13 12 11 10 09 08

Table of Contents

What Is a Thunderstorm?

Boom! Bright flashes light up the sky. What kind of storm is this?

It is a thunderstorm. Huge clouds
called **thunderheads** fill the sky.

Thunderstorms form when warm, wet air meets cooler, drier air. Small droplets of water in the air come together. The droplets form into clouds.

A thunderstorm seen from space

The clouds grow bigger and darker.
Soon, water begins to fall from the
clouds. It is raining.

Strong winds blow. Water droplets move around inside the thunderhead. The droplets crash into one another.

The crashing water droplets cause an **electrical charge** to build up in the clouds.

What happens to this electrical charge?

Lightning

The electrical charge in a cloud forms a huge spark. This spark is a bolt of **lightning**. Most lightning passes from one cloud to another.

Some lightning strikes the ground.
Lightning usually hits high points such
as treetops.

Lightning can be deadly. If you see lightning, you should stay inside. What sound goes with lightning?

Thunderstorms can be loud.

Thunder

A clap of **thunder** follows each lightning strike. Lightning bolts are very hot. They heat the air around them. The air heats up fast and gets bigger. It makes a booming sound. Light travels faster than sound. That is why we see lightning before we hear the thunder.

These lumps of ice fell in a thunderstorm.
What are they called?

Dangers of Thunderstorms

Thunder won't hurt you. But lightning strikes can be very dangerous. What other dangers do thunderstorms bring? Some thunderstorms also bring **hail**. Hail is balls or lumps of ice. Hail forms inside thunderheads. It can damage cars and roofs.

Sometimes, thunderstorms produce **tornadoes**. These dangerous winds spin at high speeds. Tornadoes can blow down whole towns.

Heavy rains fall during thunderstorms. The rain can cause **flooding**. Rivers may overflow. Streets may be filled with water.

Powerful gusts of wind can flatten homes. They can rip branches off trees.

Thunderstorms are strong and dangerous. How can people prepare for thunderstorms?

Staying Safe

Scientists watch for storms. They warn people when a thunderstorm is on the way. Most towns and cities have warning sirens. They blow when a dangerous storm is coming.

A tornado warning siren

Sirens blow when there is a tornado. People should stay indoors during a storm. Many people go into basements or **storm shelters**.

Thunderstorms are powerful. Sometimes they are deadly. But they are an important part of nature.

How Hail Forms

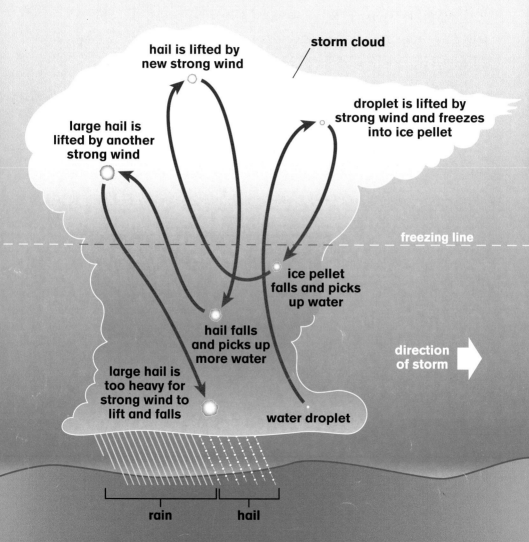

storm cloud

hail is lifted by
new strong wind

droplet is lifted by
strong wind and freezes
into ice pellet

large hail is
lifted by another
strong wind

freezing line

ice pellet
falls and picks
up water

hail falls
and picks up
more water

direction
of storm

large hail is
too heavy for
strong wind to
lift and falls

water droplet

rain   hail

THUNDERSTORM FACTS

- Thunderstorms can occur at almost any time. But they are most likely in the spring and summer during the afternoon and evening hours.

- Some people say that lightning never strikes the same place twice. But that isn't true. Lightning can strike the same place more than once even during the same storm.

- In the United States, an average of 300 people are injured and 80 people are killed by lightning each year.

- The largest lump of hail ever found fell in Aurora, Nebraska, in 2003. It measured almost 8 inches (20 centimeters) across. That's almost as wide as a soccer ball!

- Hail falls at speeds of 70 to 100 miles (110 to 160 kilometers) per hour.

Further Reading

Books

Collins, Andrew. *Violent Weather: Thunderstorms, Tornadoes, and Hurricanes.* Washington, DC: National Geographic, 2006.

Miles, Elizabeth. *Thunder and Lightning.* Chicago: Heinemann Library, 2005.

Netzley, Patricia D. *Thunderstorms.* Farmington Hills, MI: KidHaven Press, 2003.

Websites

FEMA for Kids: Thunderstorms
http://www.fema.gov/kids/thunder.htm
This site teaches you how to prepare for thunderstorms. You can also learn what causes thunderstorms, play games, read stories, and become a Disaster Action Kid.

Weather Wiz Kids: Lightning
http://www.weatherwizkids.com/lightning1.htm
Learn more interesting facts about lightning, and find lightning and thunder experiments.

Web Weather for Kids! Thunderstorms & Tornadoes
http://www.eo.ucar.edu/webweather/thunderhome.html
See what makes weather wet and wild, find fun activities, and learn how to forecast the weather!

Glossary

electrical charge: a form of energy. Electricity is the energy used to light lamps and power some machines.

flooding: the flow of large amounts of water over places that are usually dry

hail: balls or lumps of ice that fall like rain during a thunderstorm

lightning: a large electrical spark that passes from a cloud to the ground or another cloud

storm shelters: rooms built to protect people from dangerous weather

thunder: the loud boom that follows each bolt of lightning

thunderheads: huge storm clouds that produce rain and lightning

tornadoes: dangerous, spinning winds that form during some thunderstorms

Index